'Twas the night before Christmas, and all through the city Not a creature was stirring . . .

BLAM

CRASH

KABOOM

. . . Except for Bad Kitty.

Copyright © 2011 by Nick Bruel

A Neal Porter Book
Published by Roaring Brook Press
Roaring Brook Press is a division of
Holtzbrinck Publishing Holdings Limited Partnership
175 Fifth Avenue, New York, New York 10010
mackids.com
All rights reserved

Roaring Brook Press books are available for special promotions
and premiums. For details contact: Director of Special Markets,
Holtzbrinck Publishers.

First edition 2011   Book design by Jennifer Browne

Library of Congress Cataloging-in-Publication Data

Bruel, Nick.
  A Bad Kitty Christmas / Nick Bruel.
    p. cm.
  "A Neal Porter book."
  Summary: After destroying all of the gifts and decorations at home, Bad
Kitty escapes from the car on Christmas Eve and finds a new friend, who
helps her learn the true meaning of Christmas.
  ISBN 978-1-59643-668-8
  [1. Stories in rhyme. 2. Cats—Fiction. 3. Christmas—Fiction.]
  I. Title.
PZ8.3.B8253Bad 2011
[E]—dc22
                                        2010037814

Printed in May 2011 in China by South China
Printing Co. Ltd., Dongguan City, Guangdong
Province

10 9 8 7 6 5 4 3 2 1

A BAD KITTY CHRISTMAS

DUH! NICK BRUEL

A NEAL PORTER BOOK
ROARING BROOK PRESS
NEW YORK

How did she get here, you may ask yourself.
It's a very long story; I'll tell it myself.

First thing
this morning
I awoke to a clatter.
I ran down the stairs
and asked,
"What's the matter?"

That's when I found Kitty
in the midst of her caper.
She'd torn through the gifts
and was covered in paper.

THE ANGEL WAS AMBUSHED.

THE BOOKS WERE ALL BUMPED.

The Big Book of Robots

THE CARDS WERE ALL CRUSHED.

THE DRUMS WERE ALL DUMPED.

THE **E**GGNOG WAS **E**NDED.

THE **F**RUITCAKE WAS **F**LUNG.

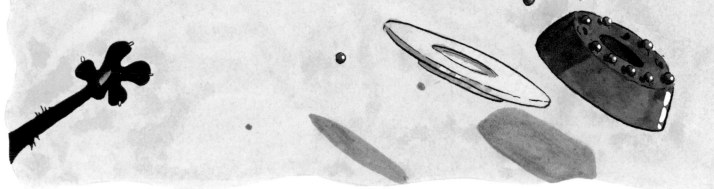

THE **G**IFTS WERE ALL **G**UTTED.

THE **H**OLLY UN-**H**UNG.

THE MANGER WAS MAULED.

THE NUTCRACKER NAILED.

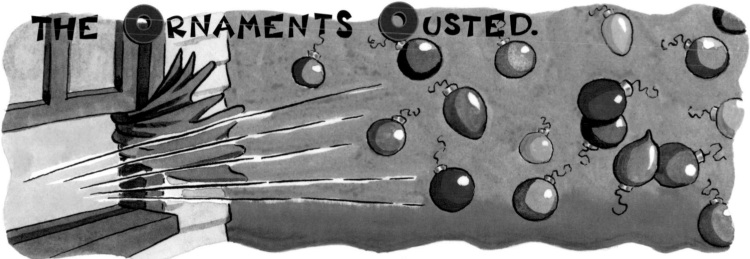

THE ORNAMENTS OUSTED.

THE POINSETTIA PAILED.

THE QUIET WAS QUASHED.

THE RIBBONS RIPPED UP.

THE STAR WAS SENT SWIRLING.

THE TREE WAS TRIPPED UP.

OUR **Y**ULETIDE LOOKED **Y**UCKY!
MY **Z**EAL HAD BEEN **Z**APPED
WHEN I HAD FOUND KITTY
IN THE SHREDS WHERE SHE NAPPED!

"Oh, Kitty! **BAD KITTY!** I'm filled with distress!
You've ruined our Christmas! Just look at this mess!"

"All of these presents, these were for you!
Why did you do it?!" And Kitty said . . .

MEW

Though there were
presents and bundles
and boxes galore,
Kitty was angry. She
wanted MORE.

She wanted . . .

AN **A**PE AND A **B**EAR AND A **C**ORMORANT DISH,

A **D**UCK AND AN **E**AGLE BAKED WITH A **F**ISH.

A **G**ECKO, A **H**ORSE, AN **I**BIS, A **J**ACKAL, A **K**IWI AND A **L**ION IN A SOUP WITH A **M**ACKEREL.

A Narwhal, an Owl, and a Penguin on rye. A Quetzal, a Rabbit, and a Seahorse in pie.

A Toad, an Urchin, a Vole, and a Whale, a Xerus and Yak fried with Zebra tail!

She was still miffed when we packed up to go
On an afternoon trip in the Christmas Eve snow.

As we left for the city to see Uncle Murray,
The window was open! And
she left in a hurry!

'Twas the night before Christmas
and out on the street,
I saw a little black cat with little wet feet.

She sat in an alley,
a path dark and scary.
She didn't look jolly.
She didn't look merry.

She looked so alone
as she sat there and pondered.
As if she was lost and unsure
where she'd wandered.

And then she began to meow
and to bellow.
She cried for a while,
until I said . . .

MEOW-OW-OW-OW-OW

HELLO

"What do we have
here? A little
black cat!
Don't you have a
home? Let's look
into that!

"There, there, little cat.
It'll all be all right.
You shouldn't be out
on this cold, wintry night.

"I'll take you upstairs
to dry off your fur.
Would you like some food?"
And this kitty said . . .

PURR

"Now, my home's a bit empty. Why, it's practically bare.
But I still have a little, and I'm happy to share."

I grabbed a clean towel to dry off her back
And set down a plate with a
small, tasty snack.

"Do you like this old tree, the one on the shelf?
Did you know I adorned it all by myself?

"You won't see any tinsel, not even one light.
It only has photos—they're all
black and white.

"Come sit with me, cat, and let me show you
All the folk in my life and the people I knew.

"Here's my Aunt Agnes
with my Brother Bobby
With dear Cousin Clancy
and his Daughter Dottie.

"That's Edgar the Elder with my Father Frank
Next to Grandmother Gail and my Husband Hank.

"These are my In-laws,
Ike and Iolanna,
With their two
Juveniles,
John and Johanna.

"They each had a Kid,
Kendra and Ken,
And the Lineage goes on
with Landra and Len.

"Here's my Mother Marge
with her lovely Niece Nan
With her Offspring Oscar
and her Partner Pam.

"That's **Quinn** in the **Quilt**,
a family heirloom.
He's **Related** to **Robert**,
who hails from Khartoum.

"That's
my **Sister Sophie** and her
Twins, **Tina** and **Todd**,
With dear Uncle Upton
who had a nose that was odd.

"That's **Vasha** my
Vriend, or 'friend'
in Afrikaans.
She's **Walter's Wife**,
and he is my son.

"This last one's my favorite. It's the whole silly gang
At a Christmas reunion where we laughed and we sang.

"We met in New York, near the end of December.
I wrote on the picture so I'd always remember.

"On here it says 'X-mas, 1962.
We're spending our Yule at the Central Park Zoo.'"

This cat looked entranced
while I patted her fur
As she stared at each
picture there before her.

"You should know, cat,
that I'm still quite content
With only this tree
that looks slightly bent.

"I may not have jewels
or a car or a yacht,
But I still have my
memories,
and that's quite a lot.

"Little cat, this is what
Christmas should be.
It's not about stuff from
a big spending spree.

"It's not about presents
all over the place.
It's not about food
or stuffing your face.

"Like Hanukkah, Kwanzaa,
and Eid, you see,
Christmas is all about . . .

FAMILY.

"Home's where the heart is, that's what they say.
So I'll bet your poor heart feels miles away.

"Don't fret, little cat. Wipe off that tear.
If we can't find your home,
then you can stay here."

But I could tell
she was homesick.
She wanted MORE.
And that's when
we heard a scratch
at the door.

"There's someone to see you,
you lucky, black cat.
I think that he knows where your
home is at."

Like a furry, black flash
she flew out the door.
She was moving so fast,
she did not touch the floor.

"So I guess you'll be leaving,"
I said with a sigh.
"I'm so glad I met you.
Tell your folks
I said 'Hi.'"

So I sat in my chair
and put my tree in my lap
And settled myself
for a long winter nap.
I was happy to know
she had a home of her own.
Too bad I'd be spending my
Christmas . . .

alone.

But just when I
started to slumber
and snore,
Again I heard
scratching
at my front door.

This cat had come back
like she had something to do.

"What do you want?"
And Kitty said . . .

MEW,
TOO!

'Twas the night before Christmas; we were filled with regrets
As we sat in our seats missing our pets.

The house seemed so empty without them around.
I wished and I hoped they were both safe and sound.

Then onto the door
there arose such a knock
I sprang from my chair
from the sudden shock.

When what to my
wondering eyes should
appear,
But Kitty and Puppy
and a lady most dear.

"They're home!
They're home!
Christmas is
saved!
Welcome
home,
Kitty!

I hope you behave.

"And thank you,
dear lady, for bringing
them back.

I hope that
you'll stay
for a late
Christmas
snack."

And she did, don't you know.
In fact, she moved in.
Some friends are like family,
and she became kin.

Up there is her photo—
It's high on the tree
Wrapped snug in the
branches for all to see.

So Kitty is home now. I think that she'll stay.
She's gone off to bed to end this long day.

This story is over,
now that everything's right.

Merry Christmas to all . . .

and to all a good night.